MW00833801

Space Cat
Kassidy

Written by Carol Krueger
Illustrated by Heath Kenny

Rigby

Ginge the cat was washing his paws.
He was thinking about the girl cat
next door, when . . .

a spaceship landed in the garden.

A door opened on the spaceship and
out came a space cat.

Dad and Laura came running out
of the house.

"Wow!" said Laura. "What a cool space
cat!"

Ginge looked at the space cat.
He knew, at once, he would not like
the space cat.

The spaceship swirled into the sky and the space cat watched it go. Then he walked up to Ginge and sniffed him.

Next, the space cat ran to Laura. He put a velvet paw on Laura's old watch. His red whiskers glowed.

"Look!" cried Laura. "My old watch is working again! The space cat has fixed it!"

Dad picked the space cat up. It purred.

"What about me!" said Ginge.

But no one listened.

Dad took the space cat inside.

The space cat jumped from Dad's arms and ran to the computer. His whiskers glowed. Words came up on the computer screen.

My name is Meep.
I like to sleep on a warm bed.
I like fish cooked for my breakfast.

"What a clever cat!" said Dad.

Then something awful happened! Laura got Ginge's cat bed and she gave it to the space cat! The space cat curled up like a furry ball in the cat bed.

Ginge had to sleep on the floor.

When Mom came home, she found Meep in the cat bed. "He's amazing!" she said.

Ginge put his paws over his ears.

Mom cooked fish for Meep for his breakfast. The space cat gobbled up the fish like a vacuum cleaner.

Then Mom put a can of cat food down for Ginge. "Here's your breakfast, Ginge," she said.

Ginge saw the space cat wrinkle up his nose.

He was .

In the afternoon, the space cat sat on Dad's knee. They watched TV.
"I wonder what's on Channel Three?" asked Dad.

Meep's whiskers glowed and twitched . . .

One,

two,

three times

and Channel Three came up on the screen.

"Wow!" said Mom.

"That space cat is smart!" said Dad.

Laura's friends came to see Meep.
They patted him. They took photos
of him.

Meep was a big hero.

The fuss over Meep went on and
on. Then one day, the family saw
a message on the computer . . .

Thank you for everything.
But I would like to go home.
Could you help me find
my red beeper?
It fits onto my collar.
I can use it to call up
my spaceship.   *Meep*

Ginge was very pleased. "I am going to
get my family back," he thought. "And
my bed!"

Mom, Dad, and Laura looked in the yard for the red beeper.

Ginge looked, too.

But no one could find the beeper.

"Meep is here to stay," said Laura.

Ginge was unhappy. He ran and hid under a bush. "It's not fair!" he said.

Then he felt it — a little cold thing in the leaves. It was the beeper.

Ginge ran into the house quickly with the beeper in his mouth.

Mom saw the beeper in Ginge's mouth. "Ginge has found the beeper!" she called.

"What a clever cat!" said Laura.

Ginge was happy. Everyone made a huge fuss over him.

Dad put Meep's beeper on his collar. The space cat's whiskers glowed and twitched. The spaceship was beeped back. Meep ran through the door and waved goodbye.

Everyone was sad to see him go.

Well . . .

almost everyone!

Narratives

What's a narrative?

A narrative is a story that has a plot (or storyline) with:

An introduction

A problem

A solution

How to Write a Narrative

Step One Write an introduction
An introduction tells the reader:

- Who the story is about (the characters)
- Where the story takes place (the setting)
- When the story happened

Step Two **Write about the problem**

Tell the reader about:

- The events of the story and the problems that the main characters face
- What the characters <u>do</u> about the problem

That space cat was a "real pain!"

Step Three **Write about the solution**

Tell the reader how the problem is solved.

Don't forget!

A narrative can have more than one main character.

We are the main characters.

We are the other characters.

Guide Notes

Title: Space Cat
Stage: Fluency

Text Form: Narrative
Approach: Guided Reading
Processes: Thinking Critically, Exploring Language, Processing Information
Written and Visual Focus: Illustrative Text

THINKING CRITICALLY
(sample questions)
- How do you know that this story is fiction?
- Why do you think Ginge knew at once he would not like the space cat?
- What sort of food do you think the space cat might have liked?
- Why do you think the space cat did not want to stay?
- What might have happened if no one had found the beeper?

EXPLORING LANGUAGE

Terminology
Spread, author and illustrator credits, ISBN number

Vocabulary
Clarify: swirled, glowed, amazing, twitched, hero, beeper
Nouns: paws, cat, spaceship, whiskers, computer
Verbs: run, sniff, sleep, watch, pat
Singular/plural: spaceship/spaceships, watch/watches, whisker/whiskers
Simile: curled up like a furry ball, gobbled up the fish like a vacuum cleaner

Print Conventions
Apostrophes – possessives (Ginge's cat bed, Dad's knee, Laura's friends), contraction
(what's, he's, here's)